# MY PLANE TRIP

## CATHY BEYLON

**DOVER PUBLICATIONS, INC.**
Mineola, New York

## Note

There are many ways to travel. Some people like to drive, while others take a bus or a train. It is usually faster to take a plane, and that is what the family in this book is doing. You will read all about Andy, William, and their parents as they take a vacation. It is Andy's first time flying, and he is very excited! He wants to watch everything on the ground grow smaller as the plane flies higher. It is Andy's little brother William's first time on a plane, too. William will probably sleep most of the time, though.

As you color the pictures in this book and read each page, you may decide that one day you would like to take a plane trip. Or maybe you already have! In any case, the book will give you an idea of what to expect, both at the airport and in the air. Have fun!

*Bibliographical Note*

*My Plane Trip* is a new work, first published by Dover Publications, Inc., in 2005.

*International Standard Book Number*

ISBN-13: 978-0-486-43982-2
ISBN-10: 0-486-43982-8

Manufactured in the United States by Courier Corporation
43982807
www.doverpublications.com

Andy is excited about his family's trip. It will be his first time on a plane. William isn't sure what all the fuss is about!

Andy packs his things for the trip. Dad is taking some of the bags out to the car.

They're almost at the airport. You can see a plane
coming in to land.

People check their bags at the counter. Each person
can carry one small bag on the plane.

Large bags are stored in a special place on the plane. The worker puts Dad's bag on a scale to see how heavy it is.

Each person walks through a doorway that has an alarm. Carry-on bags are checked on a moving track.

6

If the alarm goes off, the person walks through again.
Some people are checked with a wand.

Dad checks to see if the plane will take off on time.
It looks as if it will!

It's a good idea to get to the airport early. There is a place to sit while you are waiting to get on the plane.

9

Finally, it's time to board the plane. Usually, people traveling with children go on first.

Andy is telling everyone that this is his very first plane trip!

Dad puts the carry-on bags in the space over the seats. Mom and William sit right behind Dad and Andy.

Before the plane begins to move down the runway,
everyone has to fasten his or her seatbelt.

The flight attendant tells the people on the plane
how to have a safe trip.

The air traffic controllers keep track of the planes
as they take off and land.

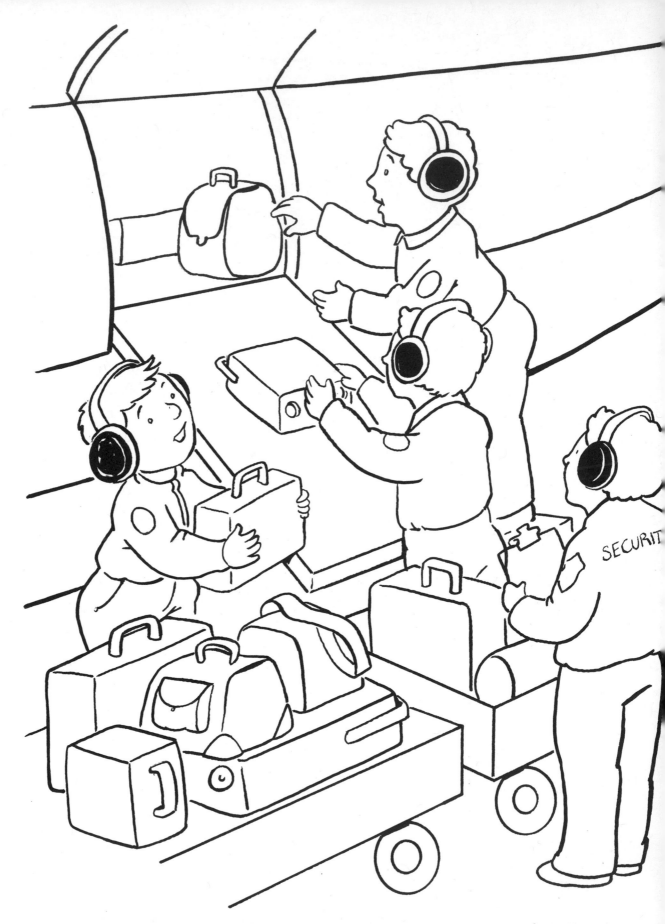

The bags have been brought from the main building
and are being loaded onto the plane.

The plane must be filled with fuel before it takes off.
A worker holds onto the pipeline.

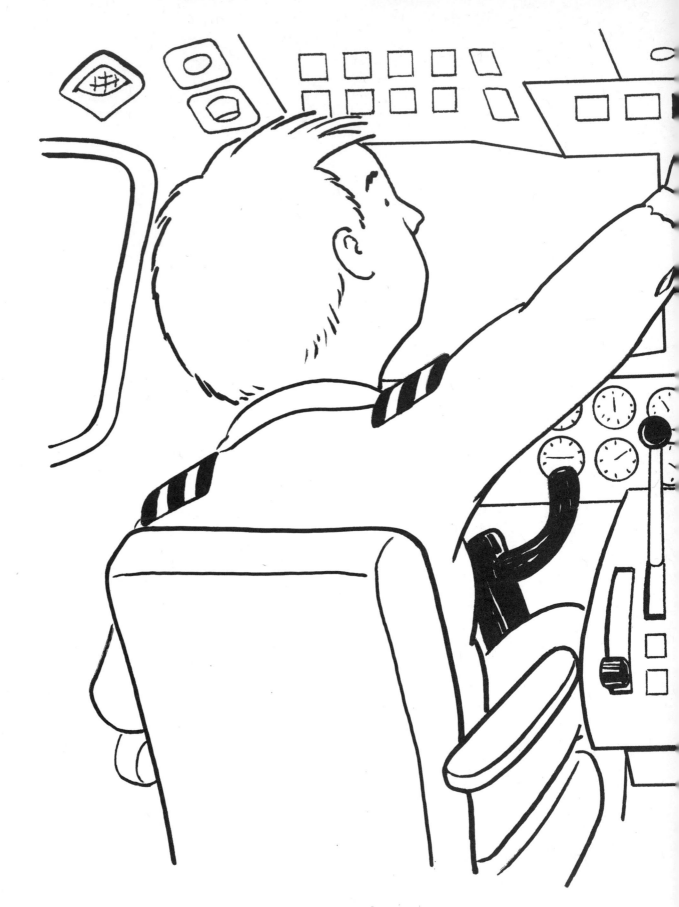

The pilot and copilot make sure everything
is ready for takeoff.

The area where the pilot and copilot sit is filled with all kinds of controls. It is called the cockpit.

The planes have to sit on the runway
and wait their turn to take off.

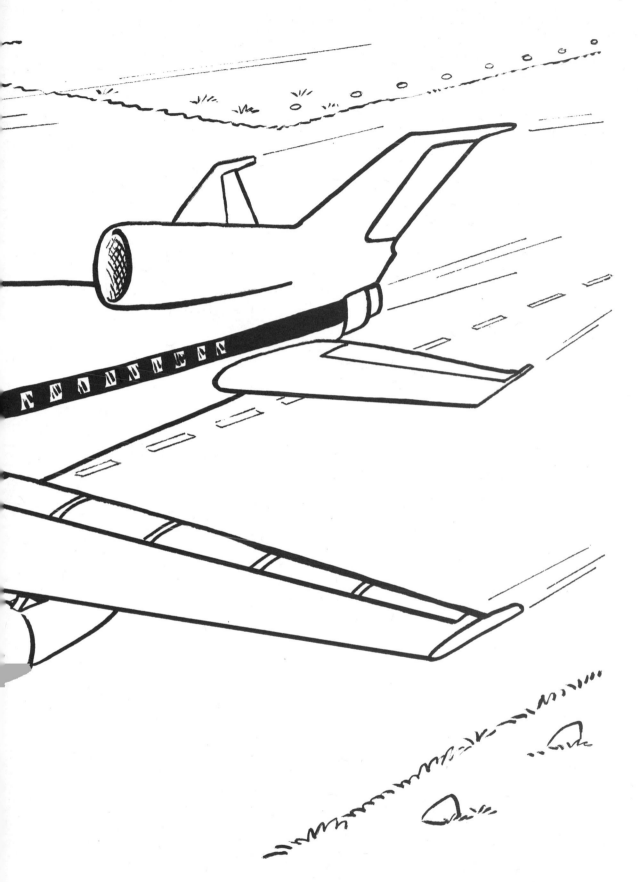

The runway is a little like a road where cars wait
for a green light.

As soon as the way is clear, the plane is given the OK
to take off. There it goes!

William is ready for a nap. The flight attendant
gave Mom a blanket and a pillow.

Andy's happy! He has made a friend on the plane.

The flight attendant gives out drinks and snacks
to the people on the plane.

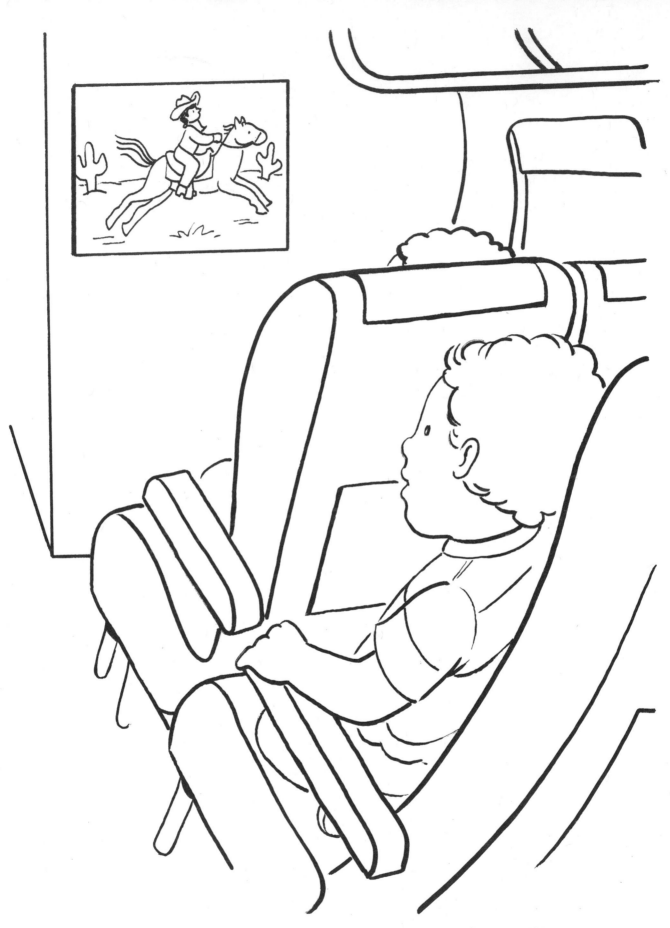

Andy is enjoying the movie. By the time it's over,
the plane will be close to the airport.

Andy sees land! In a moment, the plane will be
touching down on the runway.

While Dad gets the bags, the rest of the family keeps an eye out for the bus.

Andy sees the bus! It's time to take a ride to the place where they'll be staying.

After a rest and a quick meal, the family is ready to explore.
Andy can't wait to take another plane trip!